ADAPTED FOR SUCCESS

SPIDERS
AND OTHER
INVERTEBRATES

Andrew Solway

Heinemann Library
Chicago, Illinois

© 2007 Heinemann Library
a division of Reed Elsevier Inc.
Chicago, Illinois

Customer Service   888–454–2279

Visit our website at www.heinemannlibrary.com

Photo research by Mica Brancic and Susi Paz
Designed by Richard Parker
Printed and bound in China by WKT Company Ltd

11 10 09 08 07
10 9 8 7 6 5 4 3 2 1

Library of Congress Cataloging-in-Publication Data
Solway, Andrew.
  Spiders and other invertebrates / Andrew Solway.
      p. cm. -- (Adapted for success)
  Includes bibliographical references and index.
  ISBN-13: 978-1-4034-8223-5 (library binding (hardcover))
  ISBN-10: 1-4034-8223-3
  ISBN-13: 978-1-4034-8230-3 (pbk.)
  ISBN-10: 1-4034-8230-6
  1. Spiders--Juvenile literature. 2. Invertebrates--Juvenile literature. I. Title. II. Series: Solway, Andrew. Adapted for success.
  QL458.4.S624 2006
  595.4'4--dc22
                          2006014292

Acknowledgments
The author and publisher are grateful to the following for permission to reproduce copyright material:
Ardea p. 9 (Minden); Corbis p. 21, pp. 33 (Lawson Wood), 42 (Lynda Richardson), 43 (Pallava Bagla), 11 (Ralph White); Empics pp. 5, 40; FLPA pp. 23, 35, 38 (Minden); Getty Images pp. 31 (Digital Vision), 14 (Iconica), 8 (National Geographic), 28 (Stone), 29 (Taxi), 20 (Visuals Unlimited); NaturePictureLibrary p. 19 (Jeff Rotman), 34 (Ron O'Connor); NHPA pp. 16 (A.N.T. Photo Library), 25 (B Jones & M Shimlock), 39 (Michael Patrick O'Neill), 13 (Peter Parks); Oxford Scientific Films pp. 12 (David M Dennis), 4 (Harry Fox); Science Photo Library pp. 32 (Andrew J Martinez), 10 (British Antarctic Survey), 26 (Gregory Ochocki), 36 (Kazuyoshi Nomachi), 17 (Martin Dohrn), 41 (Photo Researchers/A H Rider), 24 (Richard R Hansen), 30 (Scott Camazine), 27 (Scubazoo/Matthew Oldfield), 22 (Wayne Lawler).

Cover photograph of jumping spider on leaf reproduced with permission of Getty Images (Stone/Steve Taylor).

The publishers would like to thank Ann Fullick for her assistance in the preparation of this book.

Every effort has been made to contact copyright holders of any material reproduced in this book. Any omissions will be rectified in subsequent printings if notice is given to the publisher.

Disclaimer
All the Internet addresses (URLs) given in this book were valid at the time of going to press. However, due to the dynamic nature of the Internet, some addresses may have changed or ceased to exist since publication. While the author and publishers regret any inconvenience this may cause readers, no responsibility for any such changes can be accepted by either the author or the publishers.

Contents

Some words are shown in bold, **like this**. You can find out what they mean by looking in the glossary.

Introduction to Adaptation

Spiders may not be the most popular animals in the world, but they are definitely impressive. Their **venomous** fangs and very strong, fine silk have helped spiders spread to every part of the world.

Spiders were among the very first animals to walk on land, about 400 million years ago. Like all spiders since, the first spiders were **predators**. They fed on the earliest insects, such as cockroaches, millipedes, and giant silverfish.

Although they have been very successful on land, few spiders live in the water. However, the water spider has adapted to life underwater.

Many adaptations

Insects are still spiders' main **prey**, just as they were 400 million years ago. However, both spiders and insects have changed a great deal since then. As they have moved into new environments, spiders have **adapted** in order to survive. Water spiders, for example, are able to survive underwater by spinning an air-filled sac called a diving bell to live in.

Insects have also changed to fit in with their environment and have developed defenses against spiders. In turn, spiders have **evolved** new ways to capture their prey. For instance, insects evolved wings to escape from spiders on the ground, but spiders adapted by developing vertical webs that could catch flying insects.

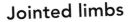

Jointed limbs

Spiders and insects are part of a larger group of animals called **arthropods**. Arthropods all have jointed legs and a hard outer skeleton (**exoskeleton**). The group includes insects, **crustaceans** (animals such as crabs and shrimps), spiders, and scorpions. Arthropods are part of a much broader grouping of animals called **invertebrates**.

Some invertebrates are large. Giant squid are a type of mollusk. This 30 foot- (9 meter-) long squid was caught near the Falkland Islands near Argentina in April 2005. It is the most complete giant squid ever found.

Packing in the species

About 1.2 million **species** of invertebrates are known. That is more than 95 percent of all living animals. Not all the invertebrates have been identified. Scientists estimate that there are between 2 and 20 million species altogether! By contrast, there are only about 45,000 species of **vertebrates** (animals with backbones, such as mammals, birds, and reptiles).

In general, invertebrates are smaller than vertebrates. Because they are smaller, they can live in many different **niches** in a **habitat**, and so there are many more species. There are whole communities of insects and other invertebrates that live under stones, a niche that is too small for vertebrates.

HOW DO ADAPTATIONS HAPPEN?

Natural selection is the driving force behind **adaptation**. Individuals of a species compete with each other for food, space, and access to the best **mates**. Some individuals are more successful than others, and these individuals survive to **reproduce**. When male garden spiders, for instance, want to mate with a female, they signal to her by vibrating her web in a special way. If the male gets the vibration wrong, or the female does not like his signals, the female will end up eating the male rather than mating with him!

Different species also compete for food and space within a habitat. Those that are best adapted to their environment and way of life survive, while those that are less well adapted become **extinct**.

5

Many Kinds of Invertebrates

Invertebrates are not a group with ancestors in common, like the vertebrates. There are many different invertebrate groups. The eight biggest groups are described below.

Sponges

Sponges look like plants, but they are actually very simple animals. Most of the 5,000 known sponge species live in the ocean. Sponges are full of small holes called pores. They feed by drawing in sea water through these holes and capturing tiny food particles in the water.

Mollusks

There are over 100,000 known species of mollusk. They have a soft body, often protected by a hard shell. Snails, limpets, and many other shellfish have a single shell, while oysters, clams, and their relatives have two shells. Slugs, octopuses, and squid have either a tiny, hidden shell or no shell at all.

Flatworms

There are about 20,000 known species of flatworms. Most of them are **parasites**, such as tapeworms, but there are free-living flatworms in the sea, in freshwater, and in the soil.

These are the main groups of invertebrates.

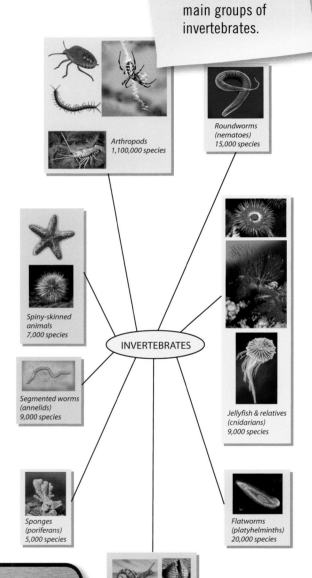

Arthropods
1,100,000 species

Roundworms
(nematoes)
15,000 species

Spiny-skinned
animals
7,000 species

Segmented worms
(annelids)
9,000 species

INVERTEBRATES

Jellyfish & relatives
(cnidarians)
9,000 species

Sponges
(poriferans)
5,000 species

Flatworms
(platyhelminths)
20,000 species

Mollusks
100,000 species

DEADLY JELLYFISH

Box jellyfish are a group of jellyfish with deadly stinging cells. They are a serious threat to swimmers at some beaches. The sting of one box jellyfish, the sea wasp, can kill a human in three minutes.

Cnidaria

Jellyfish, **corals**, and sea anemones are part of a group called the cnidaria. Most of the 9,000 species of cnidarians live in the ocean. They usually have a ring of tentacles around their mouth, and stinging cells called nematocysts to defend themselves and to help catch their prey.

Echinoderms

Sea urchins and starfish are part of the group known as the echinoderms (meaning spiny-skinned). About 7,000 species are known, all of which live in the ocean. Starfish and sea urchins are the best-known echinoderms.

Segmented worms

Earthworms and leeches are the best-known of the 9,000 or so segmented worms. There are also many kinds in the sea. As the name suggests, the body of a segmented worm is divided into many small segments.

Roundworms

About 15,000 species of roundworms (nematodes) are known, but scientists estimate there are actually more than half a million. Roundworms are found everywhere, but especially in the soil and on the seabed. Some species are parasites on animals or plants. Most nematodes are tiny or microscopic, but the parasitic roundworms that live in sperm whales can grow to 42.6 feet (13 meters) long.

Key

1. Echinoderms 7,000
2. Sponges 5,000
3. Cnidaria 9,000
4. Mollusks 100,000
5. Flatworms 20,000
6. Roundworms 15,000
7. Segmented worms 9,000
8. Arthropods 1,100,000

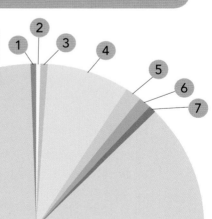

This pie chart shows the number of species for each of the main groups of invertebrates.

Arthropods

Arthropods are by far the largest group of invertebrates, with well over a million different species. Nearly a million of these are insects. Spiders are the next largest group, with 35,000 species, and there are about 30,000 crustaceans. Scorpions, centipedes, and millipedes are also arthropods.

Widespread Spiders

Most land invertebrates are not well adapted to life on land. Many of them are found only in moist habitats. However, spiders can live in just about any land habitat. You can find them on high mountains, in the hottest deserts, in the Arctic, and in other hostile environments.

Dune spiders keep their temperature down in desert environments by spending much of their time in an underground burrow.

Heat and cold

Mammals and birds that live in cold conditions have thick coats of fur, feathers, or blubber (fat) to help keep them warm. Spiders do not have this type of covering. They survive by avoiding the worst of the cold in a burrow or another type of shelter. Some spiders use silk to help stay warm. Jumping spiders that live high in the Himalaya mountain range in Asia survive cold nights and stormy weather by finding a safe hiding place and spinning a warm silk cell.

Burrows can protect spiders in hot conditions as well as cold ones. The dune spider lives in the Namib Desert in Africa. It digs a silk-lined burrow, then spins a flat web with sticky edges on the sand surface just outside the burrow. By sheltering in the burrow and only coming out when prey is caught on the web, the spider can remain active even when the temperature climbs to extreme highs.

Getting there first

Spiders do not have wings as insects do, but this does not stop them from being among the first to **colonize** new environments. Being first on the scene gives them the chance to find the best niches before there is any competition.

Sometimes volcanic activity pushes up a new island in the middle of the ocean. Spiders are usually among the first animals to reach a volcanic island. They get to new islands and other remote places by ballooning.

A ballooning spider lifts up its **abdomen** and pushes out a long line of fine silk. Then the wind catches the silk line and lifts the spider into the air. Ballooning spiders have been spotted at heights of 14,800 feet (4,500 meters) and at distances of 1,000 miles (1,600 kilometers) from the nearest land. Spiders usually go ballooning when they are small spiderlings, soon after they hatch. They do this if the habitat where they hatched is overcrowded or if there is not enough food. Some smaller spiders, such as money spiders, can balloon when they are adults.

SEA SPIDER

The marine wolf spider is one of the few spiders that has adapted to life in the sea. It lives on the seashore, catching small crustaceans in rock pools. When the tide comes in, the spider climbs into a crack in the rocks and spins a silk door over the entrance. It stays snug in its crack until the tide goes out again.

spider plugs the entrance to its beach retreat before the tide comes in.

Where Other Arthropods Live

Spiders can adapt to most environments, but they are not the only arthropods to do so. Other groups of arthropods also live just about everywhere imaginable. The secret of their success is their hard outer covering.

This enlarged photo shows a springtail from the dry valleys of the Antarctic. Springtails can survive temperatures as low as -33 °F (-28 °C).

Useful cuticle

An arthropod's hard exoskeleton (known as the cuticle) is made of a material called chitin. In the exoskeleton, thick layers of chitin give protection from injury and keep out parasites. In other parts of the body, thin layers of chitin make a flexible material for leg joints and for an insect's wings. Spiders and insects have a waterproof wax layer on the outside of the cuticle, which keeps them from drying out on land.

Adapted to extremes

The cuticle is just one adaptation that has helped arthropods colonize all kinds of extreme environments.

Springtails and mites are arthropods that have adapted to living in the dry valleys of the Antarctic —one of the most extreme environments on Earth. A special chemical in their blood acts as antifreeze and stops it from freezing at extremely cold temperatures. Springtails and mites can also survive for a time completely frozen in ice.

At the other extreme are insects called brine flies, which generally live along seashores and by salt lakes. The flies can survive at temperatures up to about 109 °F (43 °C). However, they can go partway underwater surrounded by a bubble of air, which acts as **insulation** so that they can feed in hotter water.

DEEP-SEA CRUSTACEANS

Until 1977 scientists thought that hardly anything could live in the deepest parts of the sea. It was too cold, too dark, and there was no food. However, in 1977 a robot submarine discovered underwater geysers called **hydrothermal vents** that shoot out hot water rich in sulphur and other **minerals**. Certain kinds of bacteria can live on the sulphur-rich water from these vents, and animals feed on the bacteria or on each other. Large numbers of shrimps and crabs live around these vents. Some crabs feed directly on the bacteria, while others eat tubeworms and other animals.

At vents in the North Atlantic Ocean, eyeless shrimps are very common. Although these shrimps have no eyes, they do have an eyespot on their back that can pick up **infrared** radiation. Scientists have found that, although the vents seem dark to human eyes, they glow brightly in the infrared.

Adapted to the sea

Spiders and insects are found everywhere on land, but in the ocean the most common arthropods are crustaceans. Shore crabs and shrimp-like amphipods live along shores and burrow in sand or mud. Lobsters live on seabeds, while barnacles attach themselves firmly to rocks and sift out food from the water with their legs. **Krill** are shrimp-like crustaceans that live in the open ocean in large groups called swarms or clouds. During the day they swim deep in the ocean, but at night they come to the surface to feed on **plankton**.

In the depths of the ocean, hydrothermal vents shoot out hot water rich in minerals.

Other Invertebrate Habitats

Anywhere spiders can live, other invertebrates also can live. There are many places where there are no arthropods but some invertebrates. In the ocean and in freshwater, there are invertebrate species everywhere. On land, most invertebrates need to stay moist. However, invertebrates have evolved a range of adaptations that help them survive in all but the driest conditions.

The soil that earthworms live in protects them from drying out and from sudden changes in temperature. If the surface soil gets too cold, worms burrow down to lower layers. Earthworms can also survive freezing conditions for short periods of time.

Roundworms everywhere

Roundworms (nematodes) are probably the least known of the main invertebrate groups. Yet they are as numerous and widespread as the arthropods. Like arthropods, roundworms have a tough outer cuticle. They have adapted to live in the soil, in the sea, and in freshwater. As with arthropods, there are nematodes in Antarctica and in hot springs. They also are parasites in just about every kind of plant and animal. Many roundworms are specialized to live in people. Some kinds are common only where people live in very poor, dirty conditions. However, pinworms, which cause mild irritation (itching), are common in children in many places.

All roundworms look very similar, but they adapt to different environments through differences in size and in lifestyle. Some are **generalists** that are found in a wide range of habitats. Many soil roundworms are found all over the world. Others are **specialists** that are found only in one habitat. One kind of roundworm has only been found living on felt drink coasters in a few German towns.

BUILDING THEIR OWN HABITAT

Rather than adapting to fit their habitat, corals have adapted their habitat to fit them. Most corals are tiny, tubular animals called polyps, with a hard shell or skeleton. They live in large colonies, and when they die, their skeleton is left behind. Over millions of years, these coral skeletons form a habitat where other corals and a huge range of other animals live.

Adapted to land

Probably the two best-known land invertebrates are earthworms and land snails. Both have adapted in different ways to life on land.

Segmented worms living in the sea have many bristles on their body and paddle-like feet that help them swim along. Earthworms have lost their feet to give them a smoother shape for moving through the soil. However, they have four rows of short, tough bristles. The earthworm moves forward through the soil by anchoring the back of its body using these bristles and then pushing the front of its body through the soil. It then anchors the front of its body and pulls the back of its body to join the front part.

Land snails have a thin skin that allows water to pass through freely. They need to live in moist places or they lose too much water through their skin. However, their shell is waterproof, so they often can survive even in dry conditions. They find a hiding place, then retreat into their shell and seal the opening. They can lie **dormant** in this state for several months.

When corals reproduce, they release clouds of eggs and sperm into the sea. Each egg develops into a free-living planula, as shown here.

Fangs and *Silk*

All spiders are predators. They eat a wide variety of small creatures, including vertebrates such as mice and small birds. However, the main prey of spiders is insects. Every year, spiders eat over 350 million tons of insects. That is more than the weight of all the humans on Earth!

Spiders hunt in many different ways, but all spiders use two main weapons to catch their prey—fangs and silk.

Poison fangs

All spiders have two hollow claws, one on each side of the mouth. These are the spider's fangs. In most spiders, **glands** in the head supply **venom** to the fangs. When a spider bites its prey, it injects venom into the wound.

A spider's venom paralyzes or kills its prey. The venom also contains enzymes—substances that break down the body tissues of the victim. The enzymes turn the insides of the prey into a soupy liquid, which the spider then sucks up.

A DEADLY BITE

A few spiders have extremely strong venom that can injure or kill a human. Sydney funnel-web spiders, black widows, brown recluse spiders, and Brazilian wandering spiders all have a deadly bite. However, with modern hospital treatment, spider bites are now rarely fatal (cause death).

The black widow spider of North America has about 30 close relatives in other parts of the world. Most of them are just as poisonous.

14

Different webs

All spiders produce silk. Different species use it in different ways for capturing prey. The best-known use of silk is to make webs.

Webs are silken traps that capture prey in various ways. Sheet-web spiders (also called money spiders) weave simple sheets of silk, with a tangle of silk lines above them. When the spider feels an insect crossing the silk lines, it shakes the web so the insect tumbles into the sheet web. The spider then moves in and bites its victim.

Purse-web spiders live in a burrow and build a tube-shaped web that extends out from the burrow for some distance. They disguise the silken tube to look like a root or a twig. When an insect walks over the tube web, the spider rushes out of its burrow and along the tube, and bites the insect, through the silk.

Orb web weavers

Orb webs are the most common type of spider web. The orb web is probably the most successful and efficient trap for catching flying insects. There are thousands of different orb web spiders. Many of them build webs covered in sticky silk, which traps insects that fly into them. A smaller group of orb web weavers use fluffy silk, which tangles the legs of insects that land in the web.

This diagram shows the basic steps involved in building an orb web.

(1) The spider trails out a sticky silk thread into the wind. The end sticks to a nearby branch. This is the bridge thread.

(2) After strengthening the bridge thread, the spider drops down from the middle to a third point, making a Y shape.

(3), (4) The central part of the   becomes the hub of the web. The spider lays more threads moving out from this hub.

(5) The spider connects these threads with a long spiral running out from the center to the edge of the web.

(6) The spiral thread is only a temporary framework of non-sticky silk. The spider now works from the outside in, cutting out the framework and replacing it with sticky threads.

15

Spiders without Webs

Not all spiders weave webs. Some hunt in very different ways. Some spiders hunt with a very simple web—in some cases, just a single line. Other spiders dig burrows and rush out from hiding to catch their prey. Some spiders are active hunters that chase down their prey.

A bolas spider hangs upside down, ready to swing its single sticky thread of silk to capture passing prey.

Web remains

Some spiders that had web-building ancestors have adapted their web to hunt in a different way. Ogre-eyed spiders are named for their two enormous front eyes. They hunt at night. Instead of a web, an ogre-eyed spider weaves a small, elastic net. It then hangs upside down above the ground, holding the net open with its front legs. When an insect passes below, the spider lunges down, scoops up its victim, and wraps it in the net.

Bolas spiders have reduced their web to just a single thread with a sticky blob on the end. They hunt at night for particular kinds of moth. The spider produces a scent that attracts these moths. When the spider feels a moth close by, it swings its thread around until the sticky blob hits the moth. The spider then pulls in its victim.

Other hunters

Other kinds of spider hunt without using webs at all. Trapdoor spiders dig a burrow and hide the entrance with a silken door, then sit and wait for prey behind the door. Some trapdoor spiders lay trip lines around the burrow to warn them as prey approach.

Spitting spiders produce a blob of sticky silk, which they fire at prey from a distance. The silk entangles the prey, and the spider then uses its strong venom to kill its victim.

Spiders such as wolf spiders and jumping spiders do not use silk for capturing prey. Wolf spiders lie in wait for their prey, then grab them in a sudden rush. Jumping spiders stalk their prey, then make a final huge leap to catch their victims.

THE BIGGEST SPIDERS

Tarantulas that live in the rainforests of South America are the biggest of all spiders. One species, the goliath tarantula, can have a body nearly 5 inches (12 centimeters) long and can measure 10 inches (25 centimeters) across the legs. Tarantulas are active hunters. They catch large prey, such as mice and young birds, as well as insects.

Spider senses

Most spiders live in a world of touch and vibrations, rather than sight. They have up to eight eyes, but in most species their eyesight is poor. The main sense they use to find prey is touch. Spiders have sense organs in their feet that are very sensitive to vibrations. They sit and wait for prey, sensing their approach through vibrations through the ground or through their web. However, jumping spiders and wolf spiders are active hunters. For them touch is not so important, as they have excellent eyesight.

A Panamanian jumping spider leaps to catch a cricket.

Arthropod Feeding

Spiders are all **carnivores**, but other arthropods have adapted to eating a huge range of different foods. The main adaptations were to their mouthparts, but their guts also adapted.

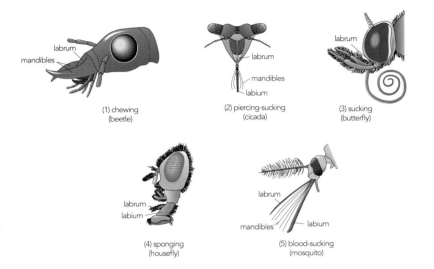

(1) chewing (beetle)

(2) piercing-sucking (cicada)

(3) sucking (butterfly)

(4) sponging (housefly)

(5) blood-sucking (mosquito)

Across insect groups the mouthparts have become adapted for different ways of feeding. These diagrams show how the mandible (jawbone), labrum (upper lip), and labium (floor of the mouth) vary among different groups.

Plant-feeding insects

Grasshoppers, beetles, **bugs**, and termites are mainly plant-eaters. Different species feed on every part of a plant—roots, stems, leaves, flowers, and fruits. Termites and some kinds of beetles feed on wood. Most plant-eaters have cutting and chewing mouthparts (1) for biting through tough plant tissues.

Many bugs feed on plant sap (a sweet liquid running through the stem of a plant), while bees, butterflies, and many other insects feed on **nectar**. Bugs have needle-like mouthparts (2) that they can poke into a plant to get at the sap. Butterflies, moths, and bees have tube-like mouthparts (3) that can reach deep into a flower.

Insect carnivores

Carnivorous insects eat mainly other insects, spiders, and other small invertebrates. Some sit-and-wait hunters rely on **camouflage** to hide them from prey (see pages 22–23). However, ant-lion **larvae** dig a pit with loose sand or soil at the edges, and wait hidden in the bottom for prey to fall in.

Other predators are more active. Tiger beetles are fast runners that chase down their prey. Dragonflies and wasps catch other insects in flight. Most carnivorous insects have biting mouthparts.

Scavengers and parasites

Many kinds of flies are **scavengers**. They eat dead and rotting meat and other waste food. Scavenging flies have mouthparts with a spongy pad on the end (4), which they use to soak up liquid food. Dung beetles feed on animal dung. This may seem unpleasant, but dung beetles and other scavengers help keep a habitat free of waste.

There are also many parasitic insects, such as fleas, lice, ticks, and bed bugs. Many of these insects feed on the blood of larger vertebrates. Most of these insects have sharp, tube-like mouthparts (5) that they can poke through the skin into a blood vessel.

Crustaceans

In the ocean, crustaceans feed in a similar variety of ways to insects on land. The main food source is microscopic plant-like creatures called algae that are found in the plankton. Tiny crustaceans called water fleas and copepods are also part of the plankton, and feed on smaller plant plankton. Some shrimps and crabs feed on seaweed and other algae.

Other crustaceans are carnivores. Snapping shrimps, for instance, hide in a burrow or under stones and shoot out when they sense prey. These shrimps make a loud snapping noise with one claw, which stuns their prey.

Lobsters and many kinds of crabs and shrimps are scavengers. Shore crabs, for instance, eat dead animals and anything else that washes up along the shoreline.

A dead, rotting fish washed up on shore provides a feast for scavenging shore crabs.

SHRIMP MOUTHWASH

Some crustaceans get their food in unusual ways. Cleaner shrimps feed on parasites that they pick off large fish. The fish do not eat the shrimps, even allowing them to clean inside their mouths.

Feeding Adaptations in Other Invertebrates

Like the arthropods, other invertebrate groups feed in a wide variety of ways. In addition to plant feeders and meat eaters, there are **filter feeders**, scavengers, parasites, and many others.

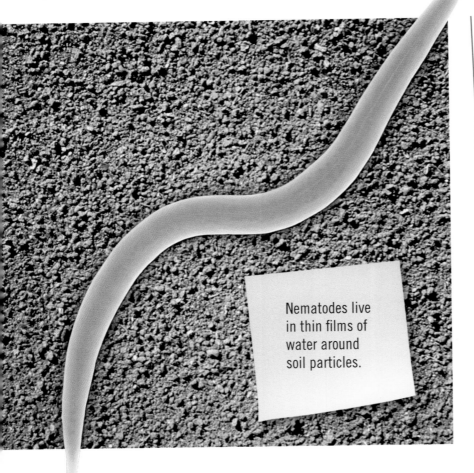

Nematodes live in thin films of water around soil particles.

Plant feeders

Many single-shelled mollusks are plant feeders. Snails and slugs scrape away at plant material with a rough tongue called a **radula**. They are pests in gardens where they eat chunks out of garden plants. In the water, freshwater and sea snails are plant feeders. Limpets also feed on plants, scraping algae off the rocks. Many sea urchins also graze on algae.

Food from the soil

There are plenty of insects and other arthropods in the soil, but also many worms. Earthworms eat their way through the soil. They extract food particles from the soil in the gut, and pass the waste out of their bodies as worm casts.

There are also enormous numbers of roundworms (nematodes) in the soil. A handful of soil may contain several thousand roundworms. About half of the soil nematodes are parasites on plants. Other soil nematodes are free-living and eat either bacteria or fungi. Free-living nematodes play an important part in renewing the soil and providing nutrients that plants need.

Carnivores

Most sea animals are carnivores of some kind. Many sea anemones are sit–and-wait predators. Any prey that comes too close to the sea anemone's waving tentacles is paralyzed by its stinging cells, then pulled into its mouth.

Most bivalve (two-shelled) mollusks are filter feeders. They suck seawater through their shells and filter out tiny food particles. Many other mollusks are predators. Whelks eat other mollusks, including clams and mussels. The whelk's foot produces chemicals that soften the shell of its prey, and the radula has been adapted into a kind of drill for boring a hole in the victim's shell.

Squid and octopuses are also active predators. Squid often feed at night on small deep-sea fish such as lanternfish, which rise up close to the surface at night to feed. Both octopuses and squid have a hard beak that they use to rip apart their prey. An octopus's saliva contains poison that paralyzes its victims. The poison of the small blue-ringed octopus of Australia is powerful enough to kill a human.

Plants and animals combined

The corals that make up the bulk of **coral reefs** get their food in two ways. Like anemones and other cnidarians, they capture small prey from the water around them with their waving tentacles. However, they also get food from within. Living in the cells of the corals are tiny algae that produce their own food by **photosynthesis**. In return for shelter and nutrients, such as nitrogen from the animals they eat, the corals get food from the algae. When two living things work together like this and both of them benefit, it is called mutualism.

Different types of reef corals grow in different shapes. Some grow in rounded lumps, some branch like trees, some are finger-like, and some form layers of flat plates.

21

Camouflaged Spiders

Many animals are camouflaged to blend in with their environment. Camouflage can work in two ways—for defense or attack. It is an important adaptation that helps an invertebrate avoid predators such as lizards, snakes, birds, moles, and shrews. However, it also can help predators get close to their prey without being seen. Many spiders use camouflage in both these ways.

A crab spider catches a butterfly. The spider's yellow coloring is an exact match with the flower where it lies in wait.

Blending in

Spider's webs are more often seen than the spiders themselves, because most spiders are difficult to spot in their natural habitat. Spiders are colored and patterned to blend in with their environment. They also use the environment to help them hide, by finding a place where they are difficult to spot and then keeping very still.

One group of spiders that have especially good camouflage are the crab spiders and their relatives. Flower spiders are a kind of crab spider that hunt by sitting on flowers and waiting for bees and other insects to come and drink nectar. The spiders match the color of the flower they are waiting on. Some can even change color slowly to adjust better to their background. Other species have a rough, bumpy body that blends in with tree bark. There is even one species that looks like bird droppings!

Good mimics

A few spiders mimic other animals, particularly ants. Ants are good animals to mimic because most predators avoid eating them. This is because ants are good at defending themselves. They live in large groups, and other ants will come to the aid of an ant that is attacked. Ants have a nasty bite, and they can spray acid at an enemy. They also taste bad.

Some spiders smell and look like ants. Smell is the most important way that ants recognize each other. The spider's disguise is good enough to get it accepted into an ant's nest as an ant. Once in the nest, the spider attacks the ants.

SNEAKY VIBRATIONS

The camouflage of a fringed jumping spider is only one of its weapons. Usually spiders of one species cannot walk on the webs of another species, but Portia spiders can walk easily on most kinds of web. They also can mimic the vibrations that struggling prey makes in a web. When the owner of the web feels the vibrations, it rushes out, expecting to find prey. Instead, it finds a Portia spider waiting to attack when its victim comes within range.

If you count carefully, you will find that the ant lurking underneath the leaf has eight legs. It is not an ant but a spider mimic.

Leaves, Sticks, and Seaweed

Other arthropods use camouflage in even more ways than spiders. Insect and crustacean predators use camouflage both for hiding from larger predators and for sneaking up on their prey. Camouflage is also an important form of protection for many plant eaters.

Blending in with the background

Most insects and crustaceans are colored and patterned so they are hard to spot in their normal environment. Some insects are truly masters of camouflage. A young katydid (type of large grasshopper) resting on a tree is almost impossible to spot because its color and patterning is so similar to the bark itself.

In the water, crustaceans have evolved a different kind of camouflage. In deep water any light filtering down from above is mostly blue. This is because the water absorbs more red light than blue light. Blood shrimps are bright red, which would not be good camouflage at all on a forest tree. In the blue light of the deep ocean, however, the shrimp is well camouflaged because it looks black.

The giant leaf insect looks just like a slightly tattered leaf.

Not just colors and patterns

In the competition to outwit prey or enemies, some insects have changed more than their color and patterning. Rather than just blending in, they truly look like other objects. The leaf and stick insects are a group of about 2,500 species, all of which look either like leaves or twigs. Some grasshoppers and bugs also look like leaves.

Flower-spike bugs look like flower petals or complete flowers. When they feed in a group on the same plant, it is hard to believe that they are not actually part of it. Mantises all have good camouflage. Some mantises look like flower stems, complete with leaves and flower buds.

ADAPTATION AT WORK

The peppered moth has adapted twice in the last 150 years to changes in its environment. By adapting, it has survived changes that might otherwise have wiped it out.

Most peppered moths were speckled gray. This made them almost invisible against the trunks of many trees. However, the large-scale burning of coal during the 19th century made the bark of many trees much darker. The gray-peppered moths became easier to see, so they were eaten by birds and other predators. However, another, darker form of the peppered moth survived much better.

In the 20th century, the air became cleaner and trees once more had light gray bark. The dark form of the peppered moth declined, and today the majority of peppered moths are once more speckled gray.

Decorator crabs make themselves look like rocks on the seabed by covering themselves with pieces of seaweed and small animals such as anemones and corals.

25

Changing Colors

As with arthropods, many other invertebrates are colored to blend in with their surroundings. However, there are some exceptions. Animals that live in the soil, for example, do not need camouflage, because it is dark underground. Smell and sound are far more important senses for finding prey underground.

This sea slug looks very similar to the anemones that surround it.

Different kinds of camouflage

Even the simplest kinds of animal can have some kind of camouflage. Many species of jellyfish are completely transparent. This makes them very difficult to see in the water. Many kinds of starfish are colored and patterned to blend in with the seabed where they live. However, sea urchins have evolved a different kind of camouflage. Like the decorator crab, some sea urchins cover themselves with grass, pieces of shell, and small pebbles so they look like part of the sea bed. The sea urchin has many tube-like feet with suckers on the end, and it uses these to hold the pieces of decoration in place.

Some types of mollusk have spectacular camouflage. Sea slugs do not have shells, and their soft bodies would make a tasty treat for a predator. One adaptation of many sea slugs is that they look very similar to the food they eat (usually sponges or corals). Certain species can change color as they move from one coral or sponge to another.

Camouflage masters

The true masters of camouflage must be the cephalopods—octopuses, squid, and cuttlefish. The body of a cephalopod is covered in special groups of cells called **chromatophores**. Each cell in the group contains a different **pigment**, and muscles can squeeze the cells to change their shape. In one shape the color of the cell is visible, but in another shape the cell's color does not show. By changing the shapes of its chromatophores, a cephalopod can change its color in a surprising number of ways.

Octopuses and cuttlefish use their amazing camouflage to creep up on their main prey —small fish and crustaceans.

Cuttlefish use their colors to communicate as well as for camouflage. This Papuan cuttlefish has turned bright red as a warning signal.

LIGHT IN DARK PLACES

Most squid hunt at night. In shallow water, moonlight or starlight shines through the water and creates a shadow of the squid on the sea floor. The squid's prey can spot this shadow, which gives it more time to escape.

Shallow-water squid have evolved a way of avoiding making a shadow on the sea floor. On their underside, they have a light organ, which produces a glow of blue light that cancels out the shadow. The light comes from light-emitting bacteria, which live in the squid's light organ. In return for producing light, the squid provides food for the bacteria.

Spider Self-Defense

Although spiders are excellent predators, they are small compared with many vertebrates. They are also attractive prey compared with insects because their abdomen is much softer than an insect's hard covering. This means that spiders have many enemies. Different species have developed different defenses against these enemies.

Burrow defenses

Many ground-living spiders dig burrows to protect themselves from predators. However, predators such as lizards and birds can dig out spiders from their burrows. Spiders have adapted by developing other defenses. For instance, one species of trapdoor spider blocks the burrow tunnel with a stone if it is attacked. Another species of trapdoor spider has a second entrance that it can use to escape when its burrow is attacked.

The Chilean rose tarantula has hairs all over its body. Some hairs can detect chemicals or vibrations in the air. Others are barbed and itchy and are used for defense.

Hairy and itchy

Tarantulas are large, active hunters, so they are quite easy for predators to spot. To protect themselves from attack, tarantulas have fine hairs on their abdomen. When a tarantula is threatened, it scrapes off these hairs with its back legs. The hairs fly off like tiny barbs and stick into the predator's face. The hairs are very fine and extremely itchy. They can be very unpleasant, especially if they get in the eyes.

Warning colors

Other spiders have developed defenses that make them less attractive to eat. One group of orb web spiders—the thorn or spiny spiders—has evolved armor as a protection from enemies. They have a heavy plate of armor bristling with spikes across their back. Any predator trying to eat a spiny spider would get a prickly mouthful. Spiny spiders are brightly colored, as a warning to predators that they are not good to eat.

Some American and Australian garden spiders are also brightly colored, with splashes of red, yellow, and black on their abdomen. These spiders do not have spiky armor, but they taste very unpleasant.

Some spiders have warning coloration but are, in fact, harmless. The wasp spider of northern Europe, for instance, has a yellow-and-black-striped abdomen, which makes it look like a swollen wasp. Wasp spiders are not poisonous or unpleasant to eat. However, most predators avoid eating them because of their similarity to a wasp.

WASP PARASITES

Wasps are among spiders' worst enemies. The wasp stings the spider and paralyzes it but does not kill it. Some species then drag the spider back to their nest, where they leave the spider as a meal for their eggs when they hatch into larvae. Other species lay their eggs inside the spider's body. When the eggs hatch, the wasp larvae eat the spider from the inside out.

The splash of yellow on the abdomen of this golden orb web spider warns predators not to eat it.

Arthropod Defenses

Like spiders, other arthropods have plenty of enemies. On land, these enemies include spiders, other insects, birds, lizards, snakes, frogs, and insect-eating mammals. At sea, crustaceans are eaten by everything from filter-feeding mollusks to blue whales. Other arthropods use a range of defenses to keep away predators.

Dangerous to eat

As with spiders, some insects have bright warning colors that show that they are bad to eat. Ladybugs, for instance, have poisonous chemicals in their bodies that make them a very unpleasant snack. The yellow and black stripes on a wasp are a warning of its sting. Many bugs are also brightly colored. If attacked, they produce a foul-smelling liquid.

The bright warning colors of these insects act as a reminder. Once a predator has tried one foul-tasting, brightly colored insect, it will avoid others in the future.

Some harmless insects take advantage of warning coloration by mimicking the colors of a dangerous insect. Some hoverflies, for instance, look like wasps, while viceroy butterflies look almost exactly like monarch butterflies, which are bad tasting. Predators see the warning colors and avoid eating the harmless mimic.

Surprise package

Other insects rely on camouflage to keep them hidden most of the time. However, if seriously threatened, some insects have a surprise that can get them out of trouble. Some grasshoppers, for instance, are dull colored until they fly. Then they suddenly expose a brightly colored area under their wings. A predator attacking the grasshopper may be distracted just long enough for the grasshopper to escape.

If an ant or other predator grabs a ladybug, it releases a sticky, poisonous fluid from its leg joints.

Body armor

Chitin is a tough material, and in some arthropods an especially thick cuticle provides armor against predators. Rhinoceros beetles, tortoise beetles, and some assassin bugs, for example, have a thick cuticle on their backs and sharp defensive spines. On land, armor cannot be too thick or it becomes too heavy. In the water, however, the water gives extra support, which means that armor can be thicker. The armored **carapace** of lobsters and crayfish is so thick that it is almost impossible to crack except when the lobster is **molting**.

Smelly defenses

Ants have several strong defenses against predators. Their powerful pincers can give a painful bite, and many ants can spray stinging acid in the eyes of an attacker. If none of these defenses work, however, ants also can call for help.

Ants do not call for help by shouting. When an ant is attacked, it releases a special smell called an alarm **pheromone**. Ants are very sensitive to the smell and follow the scent back to its source. Within a short time, other ants come charging to the spot, ready to defend the ant under attack.

Scorpions have two defenses against enemies—an armored body and a venomous sting.

BOMBARDIER BEETLES

Bombardier beetles have probably the most effective defense of any arthropod. If attacked, a bombardier beetle sprays its attacker with a jet of hot, scalding chemicals that cause blisters and burning. The jet is formed by mixing two chemicals in a chamber in the beetle's abdomen. The tip of the beetle's abdomen forms a nozzle, which it can swivel around to point at its attacker. The spray is strong enough to drive away a toad.

Other Invertebrate Defenses

Many invertebrates are small and soft-bodied. They might seem like an easy target for any hungry predator. However, a species that had no defenses would not last long in the constant competition for food and space, so soft-bodied invertebrates have developed various defenses.

A queen conch is a large gastropod with a shell up to 1 foot (30 centimeters) long. The huge shell is very heavy.

Hard shells

Many molluscs protect their soft bodies inside shells. Gastropods (single-shelled molluscs), such as snails and whelks, have spiral shells, and their whole body is twisted to fit inside this spiral shape. Bivalves have two shells joined by a hinge. Some molluscs have partly or completely lost their shells, but they have developed other defenses. Cephalopods (octopuses, squid, and cuttlefish) have defenses that work very well in their ocean habitat. If a cephalopod is attacked, it shoots black ink into the water to blind and confuse the predator. It then makes a jet-powered escape. To do this it fills its body with water, then contracts and pushes all the water out through a nozzle on the underside of the body. This pushes it forward in the water.

A STRANGE WAY TO ESCAPE

Sea cucumbers have a very strange way of distracting predators. They actually throw up their guts! Sea cucumbers can throw up most of their internal organs if they are attacked. The attacker grabs the sea cucumber's insides, but the sea cucumber itself gets away. The internal organs grow back again afterward.

Spiny urchins

Sea urchins are relatives of starfish. A sea urchin looks like a ball of prickles. The many spines sticking out from its body give it protection from most predators and help it move. Different species have very different spines. The slate-pencil sea urchin has thick, squarish spines that it can use to wedge itself into holes and cracks, so that a predator cannot reach it. Needle-spined sea urchins have spines that are long and thin, with sharp points that break off.

The crown of thorns starfish also uses spines to defend itself from predators. The spines contain a toxin (poison) that can give a human a very painful wound.

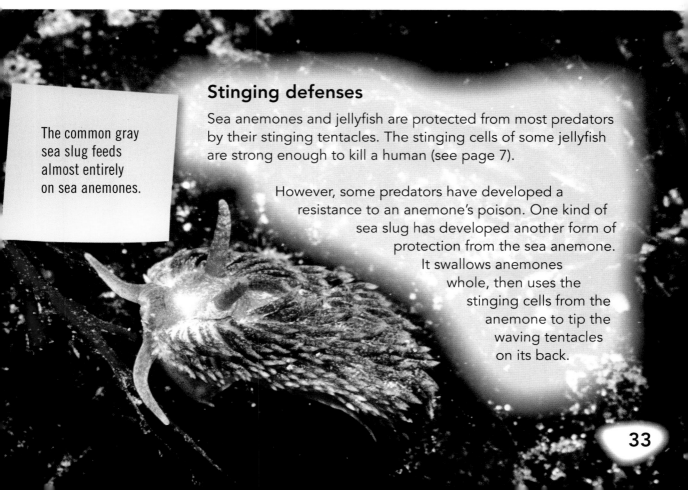

The common gray sea slug feeds almost entirely on sea anemones.

Stinging defenses

Sea anemones and jellyfish are protected from most predators by their stinging tentacles. The stinging cells of some jellyfish are strong enough to kill a human (see page 7).

However, some predators have developed a resistance to an anemone's poison. One kind of sea slug has developed another form of protection from the sea anemone. It swallows anemones whole, then uses the stinging cells from the anemone to tip the waving tentacles on its back.

Unsociable Spiders

Most spiders do not have much of a social life. They live and hunt alone. There are good reasons for this. Insects are small animals that do not make a meal for more than one spider. Therefore, there is no advantage for spiders to work together.

Meeting to mate

Male spiders are usually smaller than females. There may be several reasons for this. Most female spiders produce large numbers of eggs, and they need to be big enough to make and carry them all. Also, being different sizes means that males and females are not competing directly for the same food.

Although they spend most of their time apart, male and female spiders do meet up to mate. The females of many spider species produce a special scent when they are ready to mate. Male spiders pick up this scent and follow it to find the female.

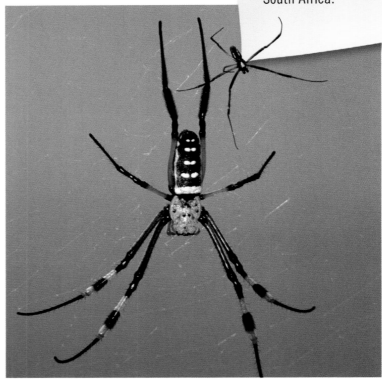

In most spider species the female is much larger than the male. This pair are Nephilia spiders from South Africa.

Going courting

Male crab spiders are tiny compared with female crab spiders. They tie the female down with strands of silk. The silk is not really strong enough to hold the female, but it calms her and makes it safe for the male to mate.

Because spiders are such fierce predators, males run a real risk of being eaten when they try to mate with females. However, different male species have evolved different adaptations to avoid becoming a female spider's meal. Many male orb-web spiders signal to the female by vibrating her web in a special way. The female then knows that a male is approaching and does not immediately attack.

Eggs and young

Once spiders have mated, the female lays her eggs. All spiders lay hundreds of eggs, but some species lay up to 2,500. The female protects the eggs with a silken egg sac.

Most spiders leave their egg sacs once they have laid them. However, a few spider mothers care for their eggs. In some wolf spiders the female carries the egg sac around with her and opens it when the eggs are ready to hatch. Once hatched, the spiderlings climb onto their mother's back, and she carries them around with her for about a week. This gives the tiny spiderlings the protection of their much larger mother for the early part of their lives.

SOCIAL SPIDERS

A few spiders do live in large groups. All these social spiders are web builders. Stegodyphus spiders build webs that are strung between two attachment points, like a tennis net. At one end of the net is a ball-shaped nest. When large prey is trapped in the net, the nearest spider signals to the others and a group quickly gathers to kill and eat the prey. Stegodyphus are small—less than half an inch (about 1 centimeter) long. Hunting in groups like this allows the spiders to catch bigger or dangerous prey, such as beetles, wasps, and moths.

All social spiders live in tropical regions, where their insect prey can grow very large. This makes it worthwhile for small spiders to work together to catch larger prey.

Arthropod Social Life

Arthropods live in all kinds of social groupings. Some animals live solitary lives, while others that gather together in huge groups. They also can have different life cycles. The lives of young arthropods can be very different from the lives of adults.

Locusts form the largest swarms of any insect. One swarm observed in Kenya in 1954 covered 125 square miles (200 square kilometers).

Living in groups

Some arthropods gather together in very large numbers. For instance, in the Antarctic summer, krill form dense swarms, with up to 10,000 krill in 35 cubic feet of water. Sometimes these swarms spread through several miles of water and contain billions of animals. Krill gather in huge swarms because of the abundance of food during the Antarctic summer, when the seas are rich in plankton. Winds and ocean currents concentrate the drifting plankton in some places, and leave other areas almost plankton-free. The krill swarms gather in the areas where the plankton is plentiful.

On land, desert locusts (a type of grasshopper) sometimes gather in huge swarms containing billions of individuals. Locusts gather when food is running out—not when there is plenty. When there is a dry spell and food becomes scarce, young locusts join together in swarms. When they become adults and grow wings, the whole swarm flies off to find new sources of food. Swarms of locusts can ruin farm crops.

A few insects—such as ants, bees, and termites—live in large organized societies in which only one female, the queen, produces eggs. In a **colony**, large numbers of worker insects are not involved directly in reproduction—all they have to do is find food. The workers gather large amounts of food, so the queen can lay many eggs. That way, the colony produces thousands of **offspring**.

Arthropod life cycles

When spiders hatch from their eggs, they are small versions of the adults. However, this is not the case for insects and crustaceans. They can develop in one of two basic ways.

- In insects—such as grasshoppers, termites, and bugs—the young look similar to the adults when they hatch, although they do not have wings. As they grow, they molt, and the insects gradually become more like adults (see diagram 1).

- In other insect groups and among crustaceans, the young larvae look very different from the adults. The larvae of butterflies and beetles eat and grow, then form a resting stage called the **pupa** before becoming adults (see 2). In most crustaceans the larvae go through several changes before they become adults, but there is no pupal stage (see 3).

DIFFERENT LIFE STAGES

Having different larval and adult forms means that arthropods can live in different ways and in different environments, at different times of their lives. This ensures that while they are growing up, the larvae are not competing with adults for the same food.

Dragonfly nymphs feed in freshwater on small water creatures, while adult dragonflies feed in the air on flying insects. Adult shore crabs are shoreline scavengers, but as larvae they drift with the ocean currents and feed on plankton.

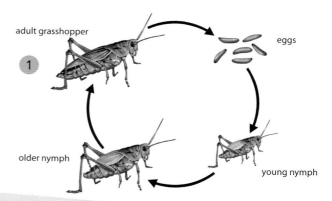

1

adult grasshopper
eggs
older nymph
young nymph

Different groups of arthropods have different life cycles.

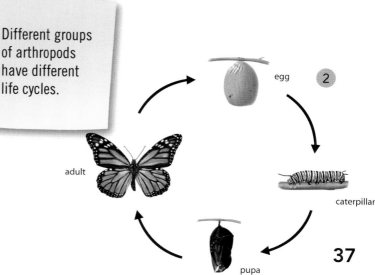

3

zoea
megalops
adult crab
juvenile

egg
2
adult
caterpillar
pupa

Other Invertebrates

Like arthropods, other invertebrates live in all kinds of groupings, from individual tubeworms to large colonies of thousands of corals. Invertebrates also reproduce in many different ways.

This is a school of squid in their breeding grounds off the West Coast of North America. The thin white objects on the seabed are egg cases.

Alone or in groups

The environment in which an animal lives may be a factor in whether it lives alone or in a group. On the seabed, octopuses can use their camouflage to hide from most enemies. A group of octopuses would find it much harder to hide than a single octopus, so they generally live alone.

In the open sea, camouflage is less effective, and there are many large predators that hunt animals such as squid. Many kinds of squid, therefore, swim together in schools. Swimming in tight groups makes it more difficult for predators to pick out individual animals to attack.

Corals living on the seabed can live alone or in colonies. Some species, such as mushroom corals, live as individuals. However, colonial living does have some advantages. In rough water, a single coral can easily be damaged by the waves. A coral colony is much stronger and less likely to be seriously damaged. Also, a single coral can only get food from a small area of water, while a colony gathers food from a much larger area.

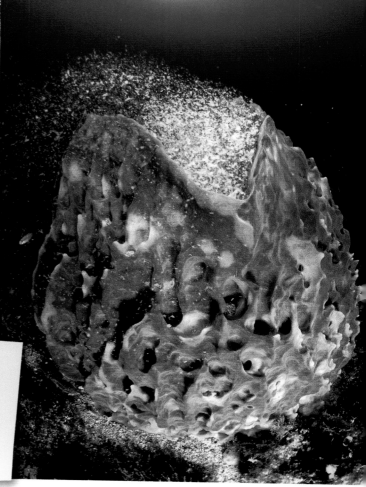

REGENERATION

Sponges have an amazing ability to regenerate (repair themselves). Even if they are broken up into their individual cells, some kinds of sponge can recover. The sponge cells join together into small clumps, and each of these clumps will eventually grow into a new sponge.

A giant barrel sponge releases a blue-colored spray of eggs and sperm. These Caribbean sponges grow taller than a person.

Invertebrate reproduction

Nearly all vertebrates reproduce sexually. However, many invertebrates can reproduce in other ways. Sponges are a good example of this variety.

Like vertebrates, sponges can reproduce sexually. In some species there are male and female sponges, but in others each sponge produces both eggs and sperm. In some sponge species, both eggs and sperm are released into the water, where the sperm **fertilize** the eggs. This is called external fertilization. In other species, only sperm are released. The sponges then take up the sperm and fertilize the eggs inside their bodies. This is known as internal fertilization. The larvae that form from fertilized sponge eggs can swim. They swim around for a while, then attach themselves to a surface and begin to grow into adult sponges. In this way, sponges are able to spread and colonize new areas.

Sponges can also reproduce asexually (without mating) in two different ways. In the first, new sponges simply bud or branch off from the original. This kind of asexual reproduction allows the sponge to grow in one place, but not to spread.

Some sponges, especially those living in freshwater, can reproduce in another way. If the water becomes cold or food is short, the sponge produces small round capsules called gemmules. The gemmules can survive cold or dry conditions. When conditions are good for growth again, the gemmules develop into new sponges.

Arthropods at Risk

Many arthropod species are incredibly successful. Spiders and insects are so adaptable that humans tend to think of them as indestructible. Insects such as cockroaches are almost impossible to get rid of in buildings. In tropical areas, mosquitoes, which carry diseases such as malaria, continue to thrive despite all attempts to get rid of them. Hundreds of different insects are pests on crops.

The Kauai cave wolf spider was listed as endangered in 2000.

Generalists and specialists

The insects that are most successful are generalists that can adapt to a wide range of different habitats and food sources. Insects that are more specialized are at risk from human activities. Several kinds of cave spider, such as the Kauai cave wolf spider in Hawaii, are threatened or endangered. This spider is found only in lava tubes (underground caves made by volcanic lava), which is a very limited habitat. **Pesticides** and **herbicides** harm the spiders by polluting the water in the caves, and construction work on roads and new buildings can bury lava caves.

Many people dislike spiders, so the extinction of some spider species might not seem like a big loss. However, spiders are important insect predators. Without spiders, the numbers of insects in the world would increase enormously.

THE INSECT TRADE

Many large tropical butterflies and beetles are at risk from traders, who sell them to collectors in rich countries. It is now illegal to collect and sell species such as the banded peacock butterfly or the violin beetle. However, illegal trading in these insects still continues.

Extinction risk

The Kauai cave wolf spider is not the only arthropod at risk of extinction. The World Conservation Union lists 553 arthropods that are either endangered or threatened. Some species are already thought to be extinct. Many of the arthropods on the list are butterflies or moths, as these are the most often studied arthropods. Insects that are found only on certain islands and insects that are specialized to a particular habitat are those most at risk.

The greatest threat to arthropods, as to all wild animals, is from habitat destruction. Each autumn, monarch butterflies **migrate** thousands of miles from North America to fir forests in Mexico, where they spend the winter months. In the summer, the butterflies are spread across the United States and Canada, but in the winter they are all concentrated in a single habitat. This habitat is now under threat from illegal logging, which has destroyed nearly half the Mexican fir forest. Many of the mature trees that the monarch butterflies prefer have been cut down, and the thinned-out forest gives the monarchs less shelter.

The Karner blue butterfly is an endangered species native to the Great Lakes region of the United States, but habitat loss continues to threaten this tiny butterfly.

Endangered Invertebrates

Scientists know very little about most invertebrates compared with what they know about vertebrates and insects. However, even among the invertebrates, scientists are aware of some species that are at risk.

The Mississippi River probably has more freshwater mussel species than any other river system in the world. However, mussels are now at risk of extinction due to pollution.

Mollusks

Many bivalve mollusks are filter feeders, straining water through their gills and filtering out pieces of food. Because of the way bivalves feed, large amounts of water pass through their gills. This means that if there are any pollutants in the water, they are likely to affect bivalves.

Over 300 different freshwater mussels are found in North America. Around 40 percent of these species are now endangered or at risk, and a few already have become extinct. Pollution is just one of the causes of the decline in mussels. Overfishing, dam building, dredging rivers, and cutting back riverside vegetation also have contributed.

Another group of mollusks that are threatened with extinction are snail species that are found only on certain islands. Habitat loss is the main reason for the fall in numbers of these snails. The Corsican snail is now limited to just 17.3 acres (7 hectares) of suitable habitat.

Coral reefs

Coral reefs have been called the rainforests of the sea. They are home to more than 25 percent of all the species living in the ocean. In recent years, scientists have found a great deal of damage to coral reefs. Nearly 20 percent of the world's coral reefs have been destroyed, while 50 percent of the reefs that remain are damaged but could recover.

The main cause of this damage is the effects of global warming. The rise in temperatures worldwide has caused an increase in sea temperatures. Corals can only grow in a narrow range of water temperatures, and in some areas the water has become too warm for the corals to survive. Pollution, overfishing (especially using dynamite to kill fish), tourists taking souvenirs, and damage from boat anchors are other causes of coral reef damage.

Specialists at risk

Like corals, many living things worldwide are well adapted to a very specific environment. This makes them highly successful while the environment is unchanged. However, when changes happen, these **specialists** cannot adapt quickly enough and they die out. The damage to coral reefs shows the risks of specialization when environments are changing fast.

When coral reefs are damaged they become bleached (white). Corals can survive bleaching for a short time if conditions improve, but more often they will die.

43

Further Information

Spider classification

There are about 38,000 known species of spider. Scientists divide them into the following groups, depending on how closely related they are. The groups are known as families.

Family	Number of species	Characteristics
Giant trapdoor spiders	83	Living fossils; live in burrows with a silken trapdoor over the entrance
Funnel-web spiders	82	Tangles of silk lines spread out from their burrows
Trapdoor spiders	114	Live in burrows with a trapdoor over the entrance
Tarantulas	860	Large, hairy; from South America; do not build webs, but hunt actively
Dysderids	480	Active hunters; rest in a small silk cell at night
Spitting spiders	157	Catch prey by spitting sticky venom at them
Daddy-longlegs spiders	779	Small bodies and long legs; make untidy webs in buildings and cellars
Uloborids	244	No venom; build horizontal orb webs
Net-casting spiders	56	Mainly tropical; make small webs that they throw over their victims
Long-jawed orb weavers	983	Orb-web spiders; include large species such as the golden orb web spider
Orb-web spiders	2,817	Garden spiders and other orb weavers belong to this group
Cobweb or comb-footed spiders	2,199	Make the cobwebs often found in homes and other buildings
Sheet-web and dwarf spiders	4,214	Small spiders, such as money spiders; produce flat, sheet-like webs
Mesh-web spiders	551	Stout, hairy bodies; build sheet webs
Funnel weavers	489	Weave silk tubes extending from their burrow. Also includes large, hairy house spiders
Wolf spiders	2,261	Widespread group of hunting spiders with good eyesight
Wandering spiders	436	Mainly tropical spiders; ambush hunters
Crab spiders	2,023	Ambush hunters; excellent camouflage on flowers and other plant parts
Jumping spiders	4,889	Active hunters; excellent eyesight and great leaping ability

Insect record-breakers

Biggest insect	Titan beetle	6.2 in. (16.7 cm); five kinds of beetle are of similar size, including Goliath beetle of Africa
Longest insect	Walking stick insect	21.9 in. (55.5 cm)
Largest wingspan	White witch moth	11 in. (28 cm)
Fastest flier	Desert locust	21 mph (33 km/h) Black cutworm flies at up to 70 mph (113 km/h), but most of this speed is from using the wind
Fastest wingbeats	*Forcipomyta* (fly species)	1,046 wingbeats per minute
Fastest runner	Australian tiger beetle	5.6 mph (9 km/h)
Longest migration	Monarch butterfly	Monarchs migrate up to 2,486 mi. (4,000 km) each autumn from North America to Mexico, then back again each spring
Longest adult life	Black ant queen	28 years 9 months (Queen was in captivity)
Loudest	African cicada	106 dB (decibels), equivalent to the noise made by a loud motorbike engine

Books

- Attenborough, David. *Life in the Undergrowth.* Princeton, NJ: Princeton University Press, 2006.
  – The life cycle of insects, spiders, and other invertebrates presented in words and photographs

- Naskrecki, Piotr. *The Smaller Majority.* Cambridge, Mass.: Belknap Press, 2005.
  – A photographic view of the 99 percent of animals that are smaller than your finger

Websites

- PestWorld for Kids
  www.pestworldforkids.org/home.asp
  – An excellent website, including information about amazing pests and fun learning games

- Saint Louis Zoo Invertebrates page
  www.stlzoo.org/animals/abouttheanimals/invertebrates
  – Lots of interesting information about spiders, insects, and other invertebrates

- 3-D insects
  www.ento.vt.edu/~sharov/3d/3dinsect.html
  – Three-dimensional animations of insects and insect information

Glossary

abdomen back section of a spider or insect's body

adapted when a living thing has changed to fit in with its environment

adaptation change that helps a living thing fit into its environment

algae tiny plant-like living things. Seaweed is an example of algae.

arthropod animal with an exoskeleton and jointed legs, such as spiders, insects, and crustaceans

bugs group of insects that are mostly plant-feeders and have long, needle-like mouthparts

camouflage coloring and patterning that help an animal hide from its enemies

carapace tough outer shell

carnivore meat-eating animal

cell tiny building block of all living things

chromatophore cell that contains pigments (colored chemicals) and gives an animal its skin color

colonize when a group of animals of the same species settle in a new location, they colonize it

colony community of animals of the same kind

coral small tube-shaped animals with a hard, chalky shell that live attached to rocks

coral reef rocky ridges in warm, shallow seas that are covered with corals and many other forms of life

crustacean jointed-legged animal with a hard exoskeleton that lives in the sea. Crabs, lobsters, and shrimps are all crustaceans.

dormant alive but not growing

evolution process by which life on Earth has developed and changed

evolve develop gradually over a long period of time

exoskeleton outer supporting structure for an animal's body, like a suit of armor

extinct when all animals of a certain species die out

fertilize when a sperm cell combines with an egg cell to form the first cell of a new living thing

filter feeder living thing that gets food by straining small creatures or tiny pieces of food from water

generalist living thing that can live in a variety of habitats

gland part of the body that produces some kind of liquid

habitat place where an animal lives

herbicide chemical designed to kill weeds

hydrothermal vent crack in the seabed where hot water and chemicals pour out of the ground

infrared kind of light below the red end of the spectrum (rainbow), that humans cannot see but feel as heat

insulation material that provides protection from heat or cold

invertebrate animal without a backbone

krill shrimp-like crustaceans

larva (more than one are called **larvae**) young of insects, spiders, crustaceans, and some other animals

mammal warm-blooded, usually furry animal that feeds its young on milk

mate animal's breeding partner; also, when a male and female animal come together to produce young

migrate travel long distances each year from a summer breeding area to a winter feeding ground

mineral simple chemical found in the earth

molt when an animal sheds its skin or fur

natural selection mechanism of evolution by which only those individuals that are best fitted to their habitat and lifestyle survive and reproduce

nectar sugary fluid in flowers

niche particular place and way of life of one individual species within a habitat

offspring young of an animal

orb web roughly circular web made of strands of silk moving out from the center and a spiral thread running between these strands

parasite living thing that lives and feeds on or inside another living thing

pesticide chemical that is used to kill insects, spiders, or other small creatures that feed on farm crops

pheromone scent chemical that animals use to communicate over distances

photosynthesis process by which plants and algae use energy from the Sun, water from the soil, and carbon dioxide from the air to make their own food

pigment natural coloring of animal or plant tissue

plankton microscopic and very small living things that drift with the ocean currents

predator animal that hunts and kills other animals for food

prey animal that is eaten by a predator

pupa stage in the development of insects in which the larva changes to an adult

radula tongue-like structure of an insect that is used for scraping off food particles and drawing them into the mouth

reproduce produce young

scavenger animal that feeds on dead and rotting animals or other kinds of waste

specialist living thing that is adapted to a particular habitat

species group of very similar animals that can breed together to produce healthy young

venom poison

venomous poisonous

vertebrate animal with a backbone

Index